Disney's Aladdin

Adapted by Karen Kreider
Illustrated by Darrell Baker

A GOLDEN BOOK ▪ NEW YORK
Western Publishing Company, Inc., Racine, Wisconsin 53404

 Library of Congress Catalog Card Number: 92-73532
ISBN: 0-307-12348-0/ISBN: 0-307-62348-3 (lib. bdg.) A MCMXCII

On a dark night in a faraway land, an evil man named Jafar and his wicked parrot were waiting.

Soon a thief named Gazeem rode up to them and held out the missing half of a scarab medallion. When Jafar fit the two halves together, thunder rumbled. In a flash of lightning, the medallion raced across the desert.

Jafar and the thief followed the medallion to the Cave of Wonders. "Gazeem, bring me the magic lamp," Jafar ordered. But the thief didn't make it beyond the opening of the cave. The tiger-god of the cave devoured him.

Then the tiger-god spoke. "Only one whose rags hide a heart that is pure may enter here!"

The next morning a poor, hungry young man named Aladdin and his pet monkey, Abu, were sitting on a rooftop. They were looking down on the marketplace of Agrabah. Suddenly Aladdin noticed a lovely young woman he had never seen before. She seemed to be lost.

She took an apple from a vendor's cart. When the angry vendor demanded payment, which the young woman didn't have, Aladdin and Abu rushed down to help her.

"Thank you, kind sir!" Aladdin said to the vendor. "Thank you for finding my sister." He quickly led the young woman away.

"This is your first time in the marketplace, isn't it?" asked Aladdin.

"I ran away," the young woman explained. "My father was trying to force me to get married."

Suddenly the palace guards appeared and arrested Aladdin. When the young woman demanded that they release him, they realized that she was Princess Jasmine, the Sultan's daughter. The guards explained that Jafar, her father's adviser, had ordered Aladdin's capture.

Princess Jasmine returned to the palace and ordered Jafar to release Aladdin. But Jafar told her that the young man had been killed.

Aladdin was not really dead, though. Jafar was keeping him alive because he had learned that Aladdin was worthy of entering the Cave of Wonders. It was Aladdin who could bring the magic lamp to Jafar. Then at last Jafar would use it to become Sultan.

Disguised as an old man, Jafar took Aladdin to the Cave of Wonders. The sleeping tiger-god awoke. "Proceed," he said. "Touch nothing but the lamp."

Aladdin and Abu gasped as they saw all the gold and jewels in the cavern.

"Don't touch anything, Abu!" Aladdin warned.

Then, just as Aladdin found the magic lamp and scooped it up, Abu touched a huge, glittering jewel.

With a loud rumble, the cave began to collapse. Frantic, Aladdin and Abu scrambled back toward the entrance, where Jafar was waiting.

"Help me!" shouted Aladdin. But Jafar refused, and Aladdin and Abu tumbled back down into the dark cavern.

Aladdin feared they were trapped forever. But Abu still had the lamp! Aladdin took the old lamp and tried to rub off some of the dust. *Poof!* In a flash of swirling smoke, a gigantic genie appeared.

"You have three wishes," he said to Aladdin. "And no wishing for more wishes."

"What would you wish for?" asked Aladdin.

"I would wish for freedom!" the Genie replied.

So Aladdin promised to use his third wish to set the Genie free. But his first wish was to be a prince—so that he could marry Princess Jasmine.

At the same time, in the palace at Agrabah, Jafar had used his serpent staff to hypnotize the Sultan. The poor Sultan was about to agree that Jafar could marry Jasmine.

Suddenly they heard the sounds of a parade. The spell was broken, and the Sultan rushed to the balcony in time to see the arrival of a grand prince.

It was Aladdin! The Genie had whisked him and Abu out of the cave on a magic carpet and had granted the young man's first wish. Aladdin was now Prince Ali Ababwa.

When Aladdin told the Sultan that he wished to marry Princess Jasmine, the Sultan was thrilled. But the princess did not want to marry Prince Ali. She was not in love with him.

Prince Ali offered the princess a ride on his magic carpet, hoping to change her mind.

During the magical journey, Princess Jasmine realized that Prince Ali was the young man who had rescued her in the marketplace. That starry night Aladdin and Princess Jasmine fell in love.

But later that night Jafar had Prince Ali captured and thrown into the sea. He wanted to make sure that Prince Ali would not marry Jasmine and foil Jafar's own evil plans.

Luckily, Aladdin had the magic lamp with him. With much effort, he summoned the Genie and asked for his second wish—to save his life! The Genie quickly transported Aladdin back to the palace in Agrabah.

Now that Prince Ali was out of the way, Jafar was determined to marry Princess Jasmine.

"I will never marry you, Jafar!" cried Jasmine. "Papa, I choose Prince Ali!"

But once again the Sultan was under Jafar's spell, and he ordered his daughter to marry Jafar.

The Princess was suspicious. "Papa, what's wrong with you?" she asked.

Suddenly Aladdin burst into the throne room and smashed Jafar's serpent staff.

"He's been controlling you with this, Your Highness!" said Aladdin.

Immediately the spell was broken.

"Traitor!" shouted the Sultan. "Guards, arrest Jafar!"

But before the guards could capture him, Jafar escaped to his secret laboratory.

Despite his hasty exit, Jafar had seen that Prince Ali had the magic lamp. Prince Ali was really Aladdin! Jafar ordered Iago, his parrot, to steal the lamp.

When Iago returned with the lamp, Jafar made the Genie appear. "I wish to be Sultan!" he demanded.

The moment had come for the Sultan to announce the wedding of Princess Jasmine and Prince Ali Ababwa. A cheering crowd gathered in front of the palace.

Suddenly Jafar appeared—in the Sultan's robes! The crowd gasped.

"Genie, what have you done?" Aladdin shouted.

"Sorry, kid," said the Genie sadly. "I've got a new master now."

The Sultan was overjoyed. That very day he announced that Jasmine could marry the man she chose. And she chose Aladdin!

And what did Aladdin do with his third wish? He kept his promise and wished for the Genie's freedom.

"Look out, world!" exclaimed the Genie. "Here I come. I'm FREE!"